For Lindsay,
who has straight blond hair and
loves all kinds of cookies

—J. C.

For Emily Stevenson
—S. S.

Emily and Alice

WRITTEN BY

JOYCE CHAMPION

ILLUSTRATED BY

SUÇIE STEVENSON

HAZAR
P·U·B·L·I·S·H·I·N·G

This edition published in 1997 by
Hazar Publishing Ltd.
147 Chiswick High Road, London W4 2DT

First US edition published in 1993 by
Harcourt Brace

Printed and bound in Singapore

A catalogue record for this title is available from the British Library

ISBN 1 874371 72 5 (Hardback)
ISBN 1 874371 76 8 (Paperback)

Best Friends

Emily looked out the window and jumped up and down. "Yippeee!" she shouted. "New neighbours! There's a girl with long, black hair and pink sandals. I like her already."

Emily ran to the front door. "Where are you going?" her mother called.

"Next door," answered Emily. "I'm inviting the new girl over for peanut butter cookies and milk."

As she ran across the garden, Emily suddenly thought, *Oh no. Maybe the new girl doesn't like peanut butter cookies. Maybe she'd rather have chocolate chip cookies.*

Emily started walking slowly. *Maybe the new girl doesn't want a friend with red hair in bunches and striped socks. Maybe she only likes long hair and sandals.*

Emily stopped walking. *I'm going home.*

Just then the new girl turned around. "Hello," she called. "I'm Alice. What's your name?"

"Emily," Emily told her. "Do you like peanut butter cookies?"

"I love peanut butter cookies," said Alice.

Emily smiled. "Then come to my house," she said. "We've got lots of them."

Emily and Alice skipped across the garden. "I like your long
hair, Alice," said Emily, as they skipped along.

"I like your striped socks," said Alice.

When they got to the house, Emily let Alice try on her striped socks.

Alice let Emily plait her long hair.

They both ate peanut butter cookies, laughed at each other's milk moustaches, and decided to be best friends.

Baby Sam

Emily skated over to Alice's house. "Alice, Alice," she called, "come outside. We have to practise our skating."

"I can't come out today," shouted Alice. "Baby Sam is sick. You come in."

Emily pulled off her skates. She ran upstairs to Alice's room. "Alice," she said, "you don't have baby brother or a baby sister. So who is Baby Sam?"

"Grandma gave me Baby Sam for my birthday," said Alice. "Come and see how sick he is."

Emily looked hard at Baby Sam. "He doesn't look sick to me," she said. "Let's go skating."

"Baby Sam is very sick," insisted Alice. "He already has a high temperature and soon he'll break out in spots. I can't leave him now."

"But, Alice," said Emily, "look outside. The sun is shining. The sky is so blue. We've got to go skating."

"I can't go," said Alice. "Baby Sam needs me." Emily thought for a moment. Then she smiled. "You're very lucky that I'm here," she told Alice.

Emily went to the bathroom. She came back with a cup of water. "I'm the doctor," she announced. "And this is special medicine. It will make Baby Sam better in no time. Now let's go skating."

"*Oops,*" said Alice. "Baby Sam just spilled his special medicine. Now he's crying."

Emily ran down to the kitchen. She hurried back with paper towels. "There, the medicine is all cleaned up. Now can we skate?"

"Not yet," said Alice. "First Baby Sam wants you to sing him to sleep."

Emily sighed and sat down on Alice's bed.

She sang: *"Go to sleep. It is late. If you don't. We can't skate."*

"Shhh," Alice whispered. "Baby Sam is sleeping. Now we can skate."

Emily and Alice tiptoed out of the bedroom.

"Now I am almost too tired to skate," said Emily.

"Me, too," said Alice. "It's not easy being a baby-sitter."

"Sometimes," said Emily, "it's not easy being a best-friend, either."

Stormy Day

Emily stared out of the window. "What a terrible day," she said. "This rain will never stop." She picked up the phone and dialled Alice's number.

"Alice," she said, "come over to my house and we'll think of something to do."

"It's raining too hard," Alice answered. "I don't want to get wet. You come here."

Emily frowned at the phone. "Alice," she said, "I asked you first. Besides if I go over there *I'll* get wet."

"If you really were my friend," yelled Alice, "you would come over!"

"If you were *my* friend," shouted Emily, "you would come here!"

Alice hung up on Emily. Emily slammed down the phone. "Who needs that Alice anyway," she grumbled.

Emily put on her roller skates. She skated in circles round her room.

But it wasn't much fun skating inside. And it wasn't any fun skating without Alice.

At lunchtime, Emily had a picnic with jam sandwiches and a jug of lemonade. But the picnic wasn't the same inside. And a picnic wasn't any good without Alice.

After lunch, Emily pressed her nose against the window. *Maybe Alice won't want me for a friend any more,* she thought. *Maybe Alice will invite a new friend over to play.*

Emily twisted her bunches, *Probably Alice called the Tupper twins. And maybe even Charlie Jones. I bet she invited the whole neighbourhood!*

Emily grabbed her jacket and ran out into the rain. There was Alice coming across the garden.

"Alice!" she called. "What are you doing out here?"

"Going to *your* house," answered Alice.

"But I'm going to your house," said Emily.

Emily and Alice looked at each other.

"Come on. Let's go to your house," said Alice.

"No," said Emily. "Let's go to yours."

Alice started to yell. Emily almost started to shout. But then Emily looked at Alice and smiled instead.

"Alice," she said, "you have a rainy head."

"You have a drippy nose," said Alice.

They looked at each other all wet and dripping, and started to laugh.

"Hey," said Alice, "getting wet is fun."

"That's only because we're getting wet together," Emily told her.

Alice pointed to a giant puddle. "I know what will be even more fun," she said. "Let's get soaked together!"